To Mom—the most amazing woman I have ever known
—W. S.

To Grandy, who means so much to so many
—L. H.

Text copyright © 2015 by Wendi Silvano
Illustrations copyright © 2015 by Lee Harper

PUBLISHED BY TWO LIONS, NEW YORK
www.apub.com
Amazon, the Amazon logo, and Two Lions are trademarks of Amazon.com, Inc., or its affiliates
ISBN-13: 978-1-4778-4974-3 (HARDCOVER)   ISBN-13: 978-1-4778-7503-2 (EBOOK)
The illustrations were rendered in watercolor and pencil on 140 lb. Arches hot press watercolor paper.
Book design by Jennifer Browning
Printed in China (R)   First edition
10 9 8 7 6 5 4 3 2 1

Turkey
Trick or Treat

by
Wendi Silvano

illustrated by
Lee Harper

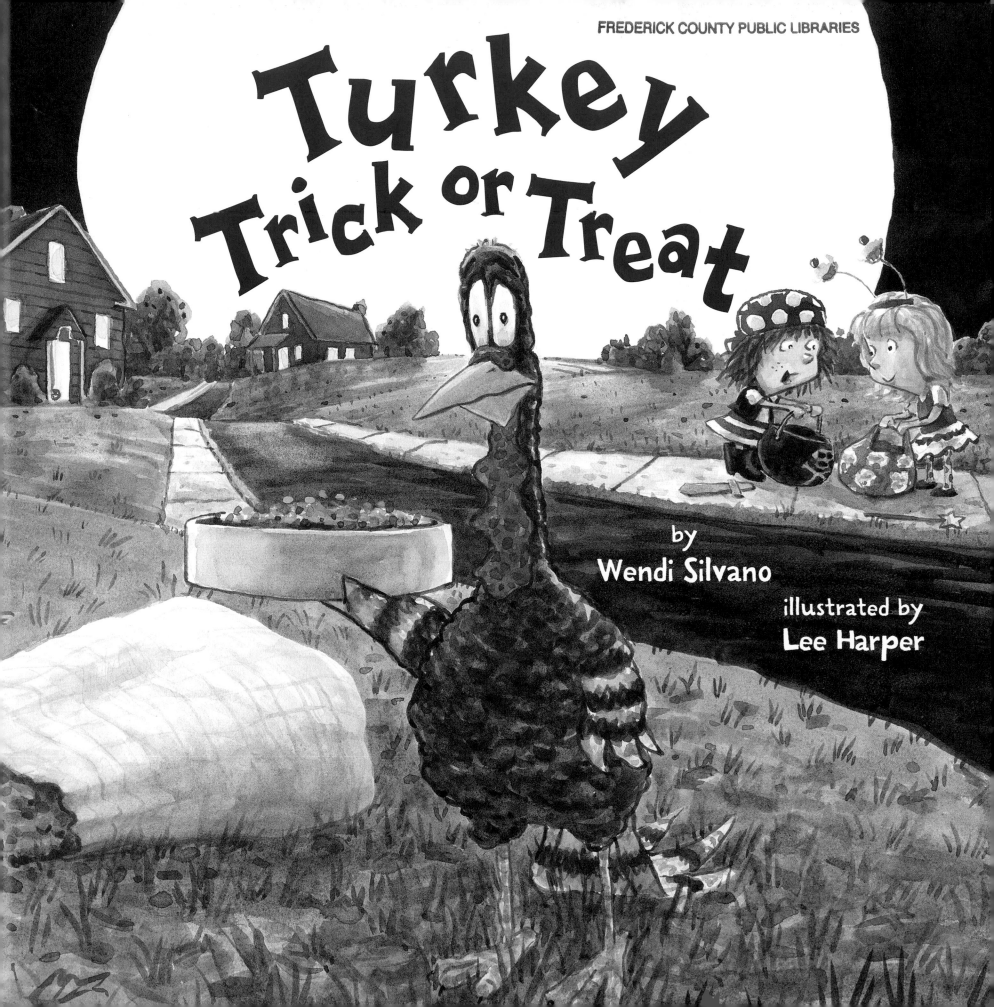

The moon was full. The air was crisp. It was a perfect Halloween night. Turkey and the other animals watched the trick-or-treaters come and go at Farmer Jake's house.

Ding-Dong.

"Trick or treat."

"Oh, you look so cute—I mean *spooky!*" said Farmer Jake's wife, Edna. "Here are some special Halloween treats for you."

Plip . . . plip . . . plop.

Edna gave out treats.
The animals all stared.
Oh, how they *loved* treats!

"Turkey is great at making costumes," crowed Rooster. "Maybe he can get candy for us!"

The animals all looked at Turkey. Suddenly Turkey had an idea. "I'll be a gobble, gobble ghost!"

His costume wasn't bad.
In fact, Turkey looked just like a ghost . . .

Turkey shivered and shook.

"Trick or treat."

Farmer Ben's son looked at Turkey. "I can see **through** this trick. Halloween treats aren't for turkeys. I'm *BOO*-ting you out!"

"Oh, gobble, gobble," grumbled Turkey.

Turkey needed a new costume.
"What now?" he asked the other animals.
Plip . . . plip . . . plop.

"How about a *baa-baa*-ballerina?" bleated Sheep.

His costume wasn't bad. In fact, Turkey
looked just like a ballerina

. . . almost.

Turkey danced all the way to Farmer Joan's house.

Turkey did a perfect pirouette.
"Trick or treat."

"Well, this trick is tutu much!" said Farmer Joan's daughter.
"Turkeys don't get treats. Go leap with the sheep!"

"Oh, gobble, gobble," groaned Turkey.
"I need a better idea."

Plip . . . plip . . . plop.

"Shiver **MOO** timbers, how about a pirate?" said Cow.

His costume wasn't bad. In fact, Turkey looked just like a pirate . . . almost.

He sailed all the way to Farmer Fred's house.

Ding-Dong.

Plip . . . plip . . . plop.

"I've got it! The *neigh-neigh*-neighbors
would love a superhero," said Horse.

His costume wasn't bad. In fact,
Turkey looked just like a superhero . . . almost.

He zoomed all the way to Farmer Anne's house.

Turkey stood tall, puffed up his chest, and flapped his cape in the breeze.

"Trick or treat."

"I don't need X-ray vision to see this trick," Farmer Anne said. "Halloween treats are **NOT** for turkeys. Fly away!"

"Oh, gobble, gobble," howled Turkey. "I'll never get any candy!"

Time was running out. The animals rushed to think of more costumes . . . but nothing seemed right.

Until . . .

Ding-Dong

Mable Mayberry squinted at Turkey through her thick glasses. Before he could say a word, she exclaimed, "Well, fluff my feathers! I've never seen such a marvelous costume. You look so real! You can have all the rest of my treats!"

Plip . . . plip . . . plop. Kerplunk!

"Treats **ARE** for turkeys! Gobble, gobble, gobble! Happy Halloween!" called Turkey.

"And treats are for pigs and sheep and cows
and horses and roosters, too," he said.

It was the **BEST** Halloween ever!